Copyright © 2012 by NordSüd Verlag AG, CH-8005 Zürich, Switzerland.
First published in Switzerland under the title *Schlaf gut, kleiner Regenbogenfisch*.
English translation copyright © 2012 by NorthSouth Books Inc., New York 10016.
Designed by Pamela Darcy.
First published in the United States, Great Britain, Canada, Australia, and New
Zealand in 2012 by NorthSouth Books Inc., an imprint of NordSüd Verlag AG,
CH-8005 Zürich, Switzerland.
Distributed in the United States by NorthSouth Books Inc., New York 10016.

Library of Congress Cataloging-in-Publication Data is available.
Printed in China by Wide World Ltd., Kowloon Bay Hong Kong, March 2013
ISBN: 978-0-7358-4082-9
3 5 7 9 · 10 8 6 4 2
www.northsouth.com
Meet Marcus Pfister at www.marcuspfister.ch.

FSC
www.fsc.org
MIX
Paper from
responsible sources
FSC® C010883

MARCUS PFISTER

GOOD NIGHT, LITTLE RAINBOW FISH

North
South

The Little Rainbow Fish couldn't sleep. His eyes simply wouldn't close. He tossed and turned in his watery bed of plants.

"I can't get to sleep," moaned Little
Rainbow Fish.

"What's the trouble, darling?" asked Mommy.

"It's so dark."

"Don't be afraid!" said Mommy. "I'll send
for the lantern fish. He'll shine his light
for you until you fall asleep. Good night,
Little Rainbow Fish."

"Could you stay with me for a while,
Mommy?"
"I'll never leave your side, darling."
"Promise?"
"Cross my rainbow heart!"

"But suppose the tide comes
and takes me away?"

"Then I'll follow you faster than a swordfish can swim and bring you safely home again."

"And suppose I lose my way
in an octopus's cloud of ink?"

"Then I'll search for you, blow
away the black cloud, and take
you home."

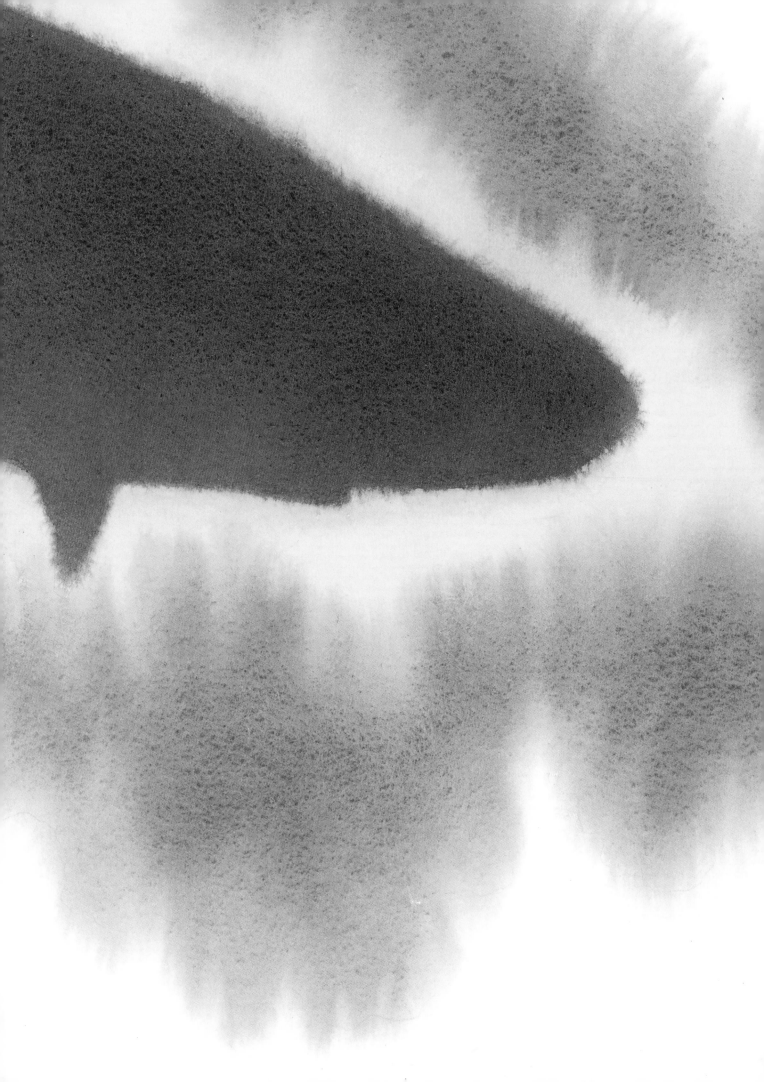

"And suppose a monster fish
comes to gobble me up?"

"Then the monster fish will have to face me first! And I'll give him such a fright that he'll swim away and never come back."

"And suppose I get caught in the
arms of a poisonous jellyfish?"

"Then I'll nurse you until you're well again, and the jellyfish will get a nasty surprise."

"And suppose I have a bad dream tonight?"

"Then I'll take you in my fins and hold you very, very tight. Good night, darling."

"Good night, Mommy," murmured Little Rainbow Fish, and then he happily fell asleep.

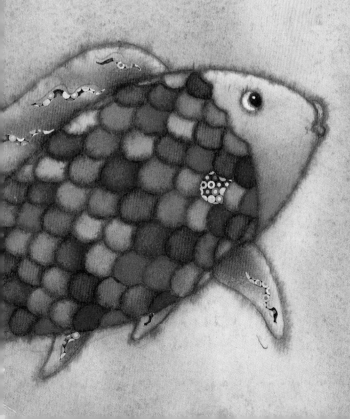